Mennonite of the Living Dead

Tim Brough

Arkady Roytman

Mennonite of the Living Dead

Story by Tim Brough

Illustrations by Arkady Roytman

Fair Page Media LLC
Springfield, PA

ISBN: 978-0-9989098-2-0

Dedication

To my ever patient husband, Joel Manon

Thanks To Cougar and Rich of Whatever Comics in San Francisco,

Ted Menten, Alan Goldberg, and David and Annette

Your community comes to your aid in a time of need . . . you share your food and fellowship.

Your community shares your hope for prosperity and good luck.

They join you when it's time for fun and excitement.

You can share the things you enjoy with the people you care for the most.

Maybe you'll just get lucky.

Communities are tight knit, social groups — groups where everyone knows everyone else, and outsiders tend to be unwelcome. Outsiders find out secrets. If there's anything more important to a community, it's the secrets.

Secrets keep the community together. If you're not part of the community, finding out a secret can get you killed. Or something even worse.

Ezekiel oversaw the raising of the new barn. Work on it started at sun-up and had been going on throughout the day. The frame, which started out simply as stakes on the ground, now stood sturdy against the skyline with men standing strong across the beams. Planks were being nailed in place to form the walls and archways that would become doors. Nails were being driven down into the fresh scent of the floorboards. It was only a matter of time until the barn would be complete and Ezekiel knew that it would be complete before sundown. He also knew that they had to be finished before darkness fell. The pounding of hammers and the humming of saws continued.

The elders were helping coordinate the work, as Ezekiel presided. Brother Jacob had been managing the workers' food, with tables spread with rich, meaty trays and friendship breads. The women were doing all the cooking, but Jacob's hearty appetite matched his laborers'. Brother Lester oversaw the materials, guiding the workers to the necessary tools and construction. He guided every board and nail to its proper place amidst the framework. Even though these men and many others were darker of beard and younger in age, none had Ezekiel's stature among the families. Each wore their black garb and white shirts with pride, but it was Ezekiel, with his flowing grey beard and wiry muscled stance, that they all gave respect to.

Meanwhile, many miles away, a group of teenagers on a senior class trip were screaming as their carts wheeled rapidly along the tracks of a wooden high-speed roller coaster. The kind of old fashioned wooden coaster that rattled so hard around the sharp curves that you think the nails should be shaking loose from the very framework upon which the rails were spiked into place. Not unlike the barn being created well beyond their thoughts, the frame of the roller coaster stood strong and sturdy. It had held the shaking and shuddering of shouting riders through many years. As scary as it might seem, and even through the shouts and shrieks, there was never any danger — just a thrill.

Brian and Susan had managed to get into the lead car. When the ride pulled into the disembarking platform, they jumped off laughing. Dave and Patty followed them out, giggling and buzzing, Patty adjusting her glasses after they'd slid down her face from the force of the ride. Joe and Meredith were squeezing each other as they got off the ride as Joe tried to act fearless even in the face of the thrills. Keith had a shared cart with a total stranger, but still enjoyed the rush of adrenaline that an old-fashioned roller coaster ride could give.

The seven teens decided that a day at the park would be a good way to spend together in the days before graduation. They had traveled from New Jersey to Central Pennsylvania to enjoy the famous theme park. Sharing the thrills and delights made for a good day, especially since they knew that graduation and coming college educations would probably pull them apart. Their friendship might have withstood high school, but they all knew that things would change after the end of summer.

Meredith ran to one of the game booths, imploring Joe to try to win her a stuffed animal. Knowing the ribbing he'd get if he couldn't prove himself as master of the game, he laid down five dollars for a handful of softballs. It took until the very last ball, but he knocked down the wooden milk bottles with a single pitch. Meredith squealed with delight and took the giant teddy bear from the carney. She hugged it tight against her cheerleader jacket that she wore everywhere, even if it was still the warmer days of late summer.

"Who's hungry?" This time it was Dave who spoke up from the group. And due to a habit that he had and wasn't able to indulge in during their stay at the park, he was obviously always hungry. Everyone laughed in agreement and they

made their way to a pizza stand. They ordered a pie with pepperoni and cheese and, to everyone's surprise, Dave fished the money out of his t-shirt pocket to pay for it. The surprise was mainly that, if he had money, it was probably being used to buy weed. But it seemed like a token of their friendship that, for a change, he'd be willing to pay for the food. It was getting deeper in the day and they were happy for the pizza. It was greasy, meaty and cheesy; almost perfect fodder for theme park fast food.

They sat around the table laughing and joking, Meredith holding the giant bear, all of them chowing down. They also took notice that their day was winding down. The sun had begun to retreat behind some of the larger rides, casting shadows across the pavement. Some of the lights and trim around the flashier rides began turning on. Keith, who would be doing the driving back to New Jersey, was more acutely aware of the time than the rest of his friends. Keith's bushy-haired brother Brian, who was still only a junior, had come along for the fun and knew that his older brother was the most responsible of the group. If anyone could get them home safely, it would be Keith.

Twilight was settling in as they finished off their pizza. Keith took the keys out of his jeans pocket and jangled them at his fellow park goers. "Let's not stick around too much longer," he stated. "It's a good two hours to get back home." He was met with mostly laughs and giggles, everyone still caught up in the day's fun, and the food.

"Spoilsport," snarled Joe, puffing his chest out to fill out his football shirt. Keith sighed. If Joe hadn't played football with Brian, he wouldn't have been along for the trip. Meredith was nice enough, but she was a blond trophy girlfriend and everyone knew it. Otherwise, no one would probably have liked Joe to begin with. Keith was not crazy about him being on the trip, but Brian and Meredith had

insisted. Keith agreed, mostly to keep the peace with Brian, but it was just like Joe to try and override any thoughts of cutting the fun off early.

All the same, Keith urged the gang to start making their way towards the exits. Joe did some alpha dog protesting but was overruled just the same. It was a late summer's day, the sun now dipping below the trees as they made their way towards the parking lot. The lights were turning on all around them, swirling like a carnival and casting crazy shadows.

Back at the barn raising, construction was complete. The doors were hinged and Brother Lester had lifted a locking board to bar them closed. The hayloft was open, with an overhanging block and tackle to raise bales to the second level. The floor was laid down and leveled. They would save painting for tomorrow when Brother Jacob and Brother Hermann could supervise in the light of day, and there was still plenty of wood and sawdust strewn around inside the barn itself. These could also be saved for the next day. Ezekiel had one more task to perform before the sun went down. The barn now cast a shadow stretching long across the fields, with the sun setting into dusk. Holding a secure board from atop a ladder above the door arch with Brother Lester steadying the ladder, Ezekiel hung a hex sign painted with the symbol of a Distlefink. "For good luck, and protection of this new structure," Ezekiel intoned, "may this barn stand strong through time and the elements."

After giving the new structure a blessing, Ezekiel climbed down the ladder and began to assemble his flock. "It's getting dark," he reminded everyone, "everyone should be in their house. Gather the children and get inside." The families hastily clustered together and briskly headed for their homes. They knew the fall of darkness meant danger, and although this ritual had been going on for a long time, few were aware of how deadly it could be. As families closed their doors behind them, each locked the door and the echoing clicks could be heard throughout the community.

Keith pulled the door to the SUV open, and everyone shuffled in to take their seat. Meredith settled the giant teddy bear between herself and Joe. Brian pushed a bag of athletic equipment under the seat to make room for him and Susan. Finally, Dave and Patty sat on the seat behind the driver. As everyone jostled to settle into their most comfortable position, Keith climbed into the driver's seat. But as he did, he began to feel around the passenger seat frantically. "What's the matter, bro?" asked Brian.

"Did anyone see an envelope that I left on the front seat?" He was ducking his head towards the floorboards to see if maybe his envelope had fallen there. He ran his fingers across the carpet and floor mats, hoping the envelope would somehow appear. "I left it here before we went into the park."

No one spoke at first. Then, sheepishly, Dave finally spoke up. "I found it on the floor, so I took it into the park." Everyone went silent, and turned to stare at Dave.

"What did you do with it?" Keith asked incredulously. "That was our gas and toll money for the ride home."

There was a brief, uncomfortable silence. Then, looking down at his sneakers, Dave began mumbling. "That's what I used to pay for the pizza," he finally replied. "And I bought some souvenirs with it."

Keith was dumbfounded. Everyone in the SUV groaned. Dave was such a space cadet that no one was really surprised he could do something like this. Even so, it left them in a precarious position. Unless someone had a fair amount of spare cash on their person, they wouldn't be able to take the Turnpike to get home. They'd have to use an alternate route. Keith cursed under his breath. There was $50 in that envelope and he was expecting to use it on gas for the ride home. Keith could use his ATM card if they could find a gas station open this late, but the turnpike was out of the question.

"I can use the GPS on my cell," Brian suggested, "and set it to avoid toll roads. It may take us out of the way but it'll get us there."

Dave hung his head and looked over his eyebrows at Keith. It was such a hangdog expression that Keith couldn't stay mad at him for long. And he was sure that somewhere along the route would be an open gas station. "Dude," Joe snorted, "who doesn't have an EZ-pass in this day and age?" Everyone turned and stared at Joe in annoyance. He flared his nostrils and stared right back.

"Come on," Keith sighed, "we're just going to have to make the best of it. Does anyone have any extra cash on them?" Everyone checked their pockets, but all came up with the same result. They had spent all their available money in the amusement park. "Brian," Keith asked, "where does the GPS tell us to start?"

"Take 743 to 322 and head east."

Keith started up the SUV and began to maneuver his way out of the parking lot. Cars were already jamming the exits lanes as other patrons had also waited till this late to start heading for home. This was going to be a long drive, Keith thought. The moon hung in front of the SUV through the front windshield. He looked at the gas gauge and knew that they'd only get about halfway before needing to fill it up. He sure hoped that one of these back roads had a 24-hour station on it. He plugged in the iPod for some driving music and started to groove to Linkin Park.

As they made their way along the back routes, Keith began to worry. All the gas stations they had passed were closed. He could only watch anxiously as the

PIZZA

fuel gauge got progressively lower. They had been on Route 322 for quite some time and, other than a few small towns, it was mostly pastures and cornfields. He checked the clock on the dashboard and noticed that it was going on midnight. If they didn't find a service station soon it was going to be pretty tight. He wasn't liking their prospects at all.

The SUV had grown quiet. Dave and Patty were resting on each other's shoulders and Patty appeared to be sleeping. Brian was awake but Susan, curled up on Brian's shoulder, was definitely out. It wasn't a question with Joe and Meredith. They were both leaning on the teddy bear and fast asleep. Joe was even snoring. "Brian," Keith whispered, "is there a gas station anywhere on your GPS?"

"Sorry bro," Brian whispered back. "No such luck."

Keith squinted across the dashboard into the dark horizon. Except for the moon and his headlights, there were no lights to be seen. The moonlight revealed little more than fences, fields and houses with their lights off on either side of the road, while the headlights remained focused on the double yellow line through the center of the highway. At that instant the red light on the dashboard indicating low fuel flashed on. "Oh crap," Keith muttered to himself. If a gas station didn't cross their path very soon, they were screwed.

"What's the matter?" asked Brian.

"We've only got a few more miles before we run out of gas," Keith replied. "If not, we're stuck out here in Bum Weasel." Keith was getting worried, as they hadn't even so much as passed a car in the last hour. In an effort to try and conserve fuel, Keith was doing as much coasting as he could. But he also knew that the SUV was a gas hog, and they were running on luck at this point. Then it finally happened. Keith didn't know how many miles they'd gone since the dashboard light had come on,

but as the SUV was climbing an upgrade, the engine began to sputter. He hoped to at least make it over the rise, and crossed his fingers that the elusive gas station would be at the bottom of the hill. As the SUV reached the crest, the engine quit. Much to Keith's dismay, the road leading down the hill was as dark as the climb up. He allowed the SUV to coast to the bottom of the slope and pulled over to the shoulder. As it had been for the last several miles, there was a cornfield on one side of the road, and what looked like a pasture off to the right.

The rumble of the SUV on the shoulder had managed to wake everyone from their collective sleep. "What's up," mumbled Dave.

"We're out of gas in the middle of nowhere," Keith replied. "That's what's up." He reached under the seat where he knew the flashlight was stashed and stepped out of the SUV. The rest of the gang opened the side doors and found their way out of the SUV. Keith waved the flashlight to and fro, searching for anything that looked like civilization. But it was obvious that the only things to be found were empty fields and the omnipresent corn. "Can someone call 911 on their cell phone, please?"

"I can't get a signal," groused Joe, "not a single bar."

"Me neither," chimed Patty. "Total dead zone."

"Well, that's just great," Joe chipped in, "we're stuck here all night."

"Get serious," replied Brian, "we can't be the only car on this highway. Someone will come by eventually. We just have to wait. I know it's hard for you, but just be patient."

Everyone stood there in silence. There was a chill in the air, and only Meredith had a jacket. She fingered her necklace with Joe's class ring dangling from it. "And what if whoever's driving this late at night is some kind of perv?"

"You watch too many movies," Keith replied. "Anybody have a better idea?"

"Why do you think all the phones are dead?" asked Patty.

"We're in Mennonite country," said Dave. "They aren't too keen on technology, and my guess is they're not about to allow a cell tower on any of their lands. No towers, no signals."

"Swell," Joe added, "we might as well be hanging out with cavemen."

"Knock it off," Dave said, in an irritated voice. "They lead a very minimalist life. It's part of their culture. Just because you don't understand it, don't put it down."

"Yeah," as Joe struck a defensive pose, "and that still leaves us stranded out here."

Keith sighed. This was going to be a long night. He checked his watch, and it was 12:30. The moon at least kept everything from being totally dark. He was able to make out the stalks of corn to the left of the SUV, a fence on the opposite side, and although he couldn't tell for sure, maybe some buildings on the far end of the pasture. He was debating whether or not to climb the fence and go knock on some doors when a pair of headlights that crested the hill began to drive towards the bottom. Brian and Dave stepped to the side of the road and moved to flag the vehicle down.

As it drew closer, it became apparent that it was a large truck, with a logo painted on its side: C&C 24-hour services. A burly man with a sharp goatee and shaved head climbed out of the truck, and asked, "So what's the problem here?"

"We're out of gas," Brian told him. "Please tell me that you're a 24-hour gas station."

"The name's Conrad, and yes, we have 24-hour gas." He looked over the crew of teenagers and chuckled. "About 20 miles away, but I can take one of you and bring you back with a couple of gas cans. Then you can get this monster to the station and fill it up for the rest of your ride home."

"I'll go," Keith volunteered, "the rest of you just stay close to the SUV."

"If I were you," Conrad advised, "I'd take your friend's advice. This stretch of highway is called The Dutchman's Triangle. We find a lot of cars here without any people in them. I've towed a few of them myself. It'll probably be safer in your car."

"You're as bad as Meredith," Joe said sarcastically. "Too many movies."

"All I know is that there've been a lot of abandoned cars along this road," Conrad warned, "with no sign of their owners. I don't want to come back here and find no one around your car. Come on, kid. Let's get going. It'll probably be close to an hour before we can get back." He towered over Keith, but in a non-threatening way, and pulled the passenger side door of the truck open. "Get on up there," he implored.

Keith jumped up to the passenger seat as Conrad hoisted himself into the driver seat. He stuck his hand up to the big guy, saying "my name's Keith." Conrad gave a hearty laugh, shook Keith's hand and said "we'll be getting to know each other for the next hour or so." As the rest of the teenagers looked on, Conrad pulled the truck away and he and Keith drove off.

"I'm not sure I like this," Susan said nervously, crossing her arms together and clutching her blouse. "It's way after midnight and I don't like being alone." Brian embraced her and replied, "They'll be back soon. There's nothing to worry about. All we have to do is stay calm and stick by the SUV. He said they'd be back in less than an hour. Nothing's going to happen."

Meredith reached into the SUV and grabbed her giant teddy bear. "I'm with Susan," she announced. "This place is just too scary for me." Joe swaggered over, and baby-talked Meredith. "No boogiemen are going to get you," he said for all to hear. "I'll protect you from the big bad dark."

Dave reached into the van and grabbed the athletic bag. "I know exactly how to spend the time," he said, unzipping the bag. He pulled out an aluminum baseball bat and glove, and pulled a plastic baggie from the glove. "This will make that hour seem a lot shorter."

"Only you could think about getting high at a time like this," Brian laughed. "But I trust Conrad. We should stay by the car until they get back."

Joe continued clutching Meredith and the teddy bear, whispering in her ear. "I can think of something to do, too." Meredith giggled. Joe took her hand and helped her jump over the guardrail that separated the SUV from the cornfield. He climbed over himself and started making his way to the cornstalks.

"Hey, where do think you're going?" Dave stopped rolling a joint long enough to ask. "We're supposed to stay by the SUV. You don't know what's in those fields."

"Sure," Joe replied sarcastically. "Werewolves from *Twilight* are just waiting for us." Meredith was still carrying her teddy bear as they parted a thatch of cornstalks and waded in-between the rows of tall plants. The full moon gave off enough light to make the green plants seem a pale grey, but still shed enough light for them to stumble their way deeper into the field.

"How far do you want to go?" Meredith asked.

"There's no such thing as too far, baby," Joe replied with a leer. "Come on. Let's try to find a level spot to lay out your jacket." Meredith wasn't all that keen on lying down in the dirt, jacket or not. But before she could protest, they walked onto what seemed like a space where the cornstalks had been trampled down to form an open circle in the middle of the field. "This is just what I was looking for," Joe announced, giving Meredith a squeeze. "It's just like it was made for us."

"Made by space aliens making crop circles." Meredith was liking this situation less and less. "Let's skip this and go back to the car."

"Come on, baby. We've made it this far. Haven't you always wanted to do it under the light of the silvery moon?" Dave even went as far as to sing the last part of his come-on line, which was enough to make Meredith giggle. She sat the teddy bear in the middle of the circle, and peeled her jacket away to rest on across the flattened stalks. She sat down on the jacket while Joe knelt next to her. "See, baby? No werewolves. No space aliens. Just us." He let his hand cup the hem of Meredith's skirt and slide it up just a fraction. "Just us, here, with nothing but corn plants."

Meredith let herself lean back and felt Joe's hands work their way up and under her clothes. His fingers touched the bottom of her panties, causing her to sigh and rest back onto the ground. Joe fumbled with his belt and tried to get his pants open, in a move that seemed almost comical to Meredith. She reached over and pulled the teddy bear between them. "Maybe Mr. Bear could lend you a hand."

But Joe was ready now. He gave Meredith's panties a pull down and slid himself onto the space on the stalks between her legs. His actions somehow wedged the teddy bear between the two of them, making it almost look like some sort of freakish three-way was about to commence. That was when Meredith thought she heard something outside the crop circle. "Did you hear that?" she whispered.

Joe was already too absorbed to notice

anything other than his urges. "Just the wind," he muttered, as he positioned himself with his arms astride Meredith and her legs wide and skirt hitched up. He slid his way to where he was close to entry, but Meredith stalled him again.

"No, this time I really heard something. And it wasn't the goddamn wind."

By now, Joe was frustrated enough not to want any further distractions. He pressed himself against Meredith and the giant teddy bear, getting where he wanted to go. But that was when Meredith screamed.

From out of the edge of the corn circle, a huge scythe came arcing down with enough force to slice deep into Joe's back. He gasped in surprise and was lifted off Meredith when the unseen attacker withdrew the scythe, pulling it upward for another strike. With a sickening crack, the blade entered Joe and broke through the front of his shirt, cutting into the teddy bear still resting on Meredith's chest.

Clutching the bear, Meredith rolled out from under Joe, who was spurting blood from his chest as whatever was carrying the scythe entered the corn circle. Meredith could see that he wasn't alone. There was a crowd fumbling into the circle and heading for Joe. Still grasping the bear, Meredith rolled away, wrapped in her jacket. She stumbled to her feet as she watched the mob set upon Joe and begin to tear his body apart. She felt like she was about to vomit as she heard the tearing of arms and legs, seeing limbs separate from Joe's body, but gathered her senses long enough to run into the cornfield as fast as she could. The rows and stalks were slashing at her as she raced in a panic to get away from the unholy sounds coming from behind her. Her sense of direction was completely lost and she could only lunge past the plants and rows in any angle that took her away from what she'd just witnessed.

When she finally ran out of breath and stopped, she could feel the cuts along her arms and face from racing through the cornstalks. She knelt to the ground, listening intently to make sure that whoever it was had stabbed Joe hadn't followed her. She was breathing heavily, still able to hear the horrible sounds that were coming from where Joe had been slaughtered. That was when she suddenly realized that she had her jacket and the teddy bear in a death grip since she'd made her escape. She took a look at the bear, and realized that there was a huge gash in its chest where the scythe had cut through Joe; the stuffed animal between the two of them had likely saved her from being stabbed to death along with him. There was stuffing hanging out of the slice, and Meredith suddenly realized that the whole thing was soaked with Joe's blood. So was her jacket. The coppery smell of it reached her nostrils and made her recoil. That was when she finally let out a scream, dropping both objects to the ground in horror.

Ezekiel heard the girl's cries. He was standing just outside the crop circle as his clan feasted on the boy. He saw the girl run, but was unworried. He'd seen the vehicle broken down by the roadside and the group of children surrounding it. Their time would come soon enough. His clan needed to eat tonight, and he knew these fields batter than almost anyone in his community. They'd follow his lead, as they did any night when meat was available. Otherwise, he'd have to sacrifice more of the community's chickens or cattle to keep his living community at peace.

His flock numbered twenty-one, of varying ages. It had started five years ago when the Schelzel children had broken open a sinkhole and had fallen into the limestone cave underneath while playing in the fields. The caves closer to the community had once been marked as fallout shelters, but what few knew was the Army had used deeper recesses in the caves to store their deadly chemicals. Ezekiel had served his country, even though he could have

received a deferral on religious grounds. He knew about the storage, and also knew its secret.

Even after coming home from the Great War, he'd kept that dark secret. The canisters stored under the earth were a kind of chemical meant to destroy the brains of whomever it came into contact with. But the weapon had failed. Not only did it not kill its targets on contact, their brains somehow revived themselves after they had 'died.' He'd seen the horrors of its use while in Asia, as his men had to kill this new enemy with bayonets to the head. You could shoot them, but they'd just keep coming unless you took a clean headshot. If they got to you and managed to bite your flesh, their saliva would turn you into one of them. Not right away, but over a period of several hours. And somehow, they'd keep just enough memory not to attack their own, but still remain in some sort of unholy unit cohesion to attack the enemy.

Ezekiel had seen it himself. The infected soldiers had fallen into a formation and set upon them, as if some sort of residual memory directed them to be loyal warriors, taking orders, still at war. They didn't attack each other, but they had somehow lost the part of their training to keep and fire their weapons. It took just a couple of encounters with these mutant half troops (and their costly decimation) for the order to come down that the gas canisters were not only never to be used again, but never to be spoken of. It was only when the Top Brass had called Ezekiel to stateside headquarters years later that they informed him of their plans to entomb the remaining supply of the chemicals in the caves near his community, and he was tasked with concealing their existence.

This he had done until the fateful day the Schelzel boys crashed through the ground and somehow exposed themselves to Ezekiel's secret. When they came home to the village, they explained that they'd fallen into the caves and landed inside some sort of chamber. They didn't even complain of feeling ill, only that they were dirtied from climbing out of the depths of the sinkhole. They were scolded for being careless, but hours later the boys began attacking their parents, their siblings and soon, their neighbors. That's when Ezekiel realized what had happened, and that he needed to get the infected away from the rest of the community. He also recalled the troops on the field of battle, still acting as if under orders. Along with other members of the village, Ezekiel managed to corral the infected into a barn where he locked them inside. He knew what he had to do. He had to appeal to what little identity they clung to. They needed, Ezekiel knew, to be commanded.

Standing above them, with scythe in hand, Ezekiel waved it over his infected clan. "You will listen," he bellowed from above. "You will be safe if you obey me! I will keep you safe, but you have to stay in your community. You must hide in the caves in the daylight and only come out at night. I will make certain you are fed and protected, but you must not set yourself upon your neighbors!" He realized that the group had stopped shuffling about the barn floor and were looking up to him and the sound of his voice. "If you do not do as I say," he paused and raised his scythe in the air, appealing to what he knew each of them feared the most, even before becoming infected, "you will be shunned. You'll never be allowed back into the community. No contact, ever again, with your friends, your neighbors or your family!" There was a low moan from the assembled, as if they comprehended. "You are Mennonite, and we protect our own!" There was a resounding, guttural roar from below. They understood the patriarch of their village. They would, Ezekiel knew, follow his leadership.

Susan thought she heard a scream from the cornfields. Grabbing Brian's polo shirt in fear, she whispered, "Did you hear that?" When Joe took Meredith into the corn, Susan was nervous about the two of them going off alone. Brian seemed unphased.

"Joe probably is pulling tricks on her," he replied. "He's such a jerk sometimes." Susan remained unconvinced. The scream she'd heard didn't sound like a practical joke scream. She also was perturbed that no one else had seemed to hear anything, or at least acknowledge something was wrong. Susan was also disconcerted by the fact that Dave and Patty were getting high while Brian was acting like being stranded in the middle of the night along an abandoned roadside was the most normal thing in the world. Why couldn't she get anyone to recognize just how frightening this all felt to her? Especially Brian. Isn't that what boyfriends are for?

It scared her all the more when, after she was certain she'd heard Meredith scream, no other sounds followed. If Joe was being such a dick, the scream would surely have been followed by a laugh or at least another sound, like Meredith yelling at Joe to tell him off. The silence surrounding them was nearly as frightening as the scream she was certain she had heard. Casting a glance at Dave, she went over to where he and Patty were sitting on the guardrail, staring blissfully at the full moon.

"Didn't you hear anything?" she demanded of the pair. She glowered at them, feeling a sort of fury at their lack of awareness. For the first time, Susan began to feel angry that Dave had picked up the envelope that Keith had stashed for the trip home.

"You need to just chill out," Dave responded. "Keith is with that man in the truck, and he'll take care of everything."

"He's good at that," Patty chimed in.

"He's cleaning up your mess! That's what he's good at!" Susan had finally reached her snapping point. Something weird was happening and only she seemed to have a clue as to what was going on. She unleashed on Dave and Patty, as Brian ran over to try and calm her. "We wouldn't be trapped out here like *Children of The Corn* if you hadn't stolen that money!"

Brian wrapped his arms around Susan, trying to hug her back into calm. But it was too late for that, as she was at full steam and not about to be pacified. "We'd be on the Turnpike and across the freaking Delaware River by now! All because you wanted pizza money!" Doing his best to try and keep the situation from escalating, Brian turned Susan around in his arms and whispered that everything would be OK, that Keith and Conrad would be back soon and they'd be on their way home.

However, Susan's explosion had soured Dave's mellowness. "Keith was over it, why can't you be? It's just a farm. There's nothing here except for corn and cows." He took Patty's arm and led her away from the SUV. "Come on, Pat," he said as they walked along the roadside. "We don't need this kind of negativity." Patty, who was self-conscious about her plain looks, always felt insecure when the girls she considered attractive chastised her. Dave never made her feel that way. She locked her arm with his as they strolled along the shoulder and away from Brian and Susan. Maybe another 100 yards or so down the road was a concrete barrier that sat atop a drainage pipe, probably for taking the runoff from the corn field and passing it along to the opposite side of the road. Dave sat his baggie down and pulled himself onto the concrete's edge. Patty did the same, as Dave laid out a pair of fresh papers. Tapping his stash into the papers, he began the ritual of rolling a fresh pair of joints.

That's when, with a crash, Meredith burst from between the rows of corn and spotted Dave and Patty on the barrier. Meredith was still hyperventilating from her panicked lunging through the maze of corn rows before finally breaking through to the roadway. Gasping, she tried to scream at Dave and Patty. "Something... killed...Joe...something...tried...to...kill... me," she pushed out between hysterical sobs and sucking in desperate mouthfuls of air. She was still gripping the bloody teddy bear and her jacket. Staggering, she kept trying to get Dave and Patty's attention.

Dave had just sparked his joint when he heard the strangled cries from Meredith. Turning towards the sounds, he saw the bloodied jacket and bear, and for a moment wondered if he was having illusions from his high. But when Patty turned and saw Meredith as well, she dropped her joint and froze in fear. Meredith lurched up the roadside to the culvert, barely able to speak coherently as she grabbed Dave and began screaming. "It tried to kill me! There's something in there and it tried to kill me!"

Patty grabbed Meredith by the shoulders and tried to get her to stop being hysterical, at least enough so that she and Dave could understand what Meredith was trying to tell them. But the blood-soaked jacket and teddy bear already indicated that something had gone horribly wrong with Joe in the cornfield. Dave managed to get Meredith to a point where she was coherent enough to explain what she'd seen in the field. "They were tearing Joe apart," she wailed. "I ran and couldn't look back! We've got to get out of here!" Finally, Meredith broke into uncontrollable sobbing, falling into Dave's arms, the blood of the bear smearing into his t-shirt.

Patty stepped back from the culvert. Absorbing Meredith's story of Joe being stabbed and attacked by a mob in the corn field was proving to be a hard swallow. She stood there by the field, mute, as Meredith just kept crying and shaking against Dave's chest. Working up the nerve to say something, again feeling her insecurity as Meredith clung to her boyfriend, she looked at the two of them and said, in a hushed tone, "Dave, we ought to at least get her to the car. I'll grab our stuff and we'll go back." She began inching closer to her friends, stopping at the edge of the culvert to pick up Dave's stash. "It'll be safer with Susan and Brian." Collecting the paraphernalia, Dave and Meredith suddenly saw the scythe as it swung from out of the edge of the corn rows and caught Patty at her waist.

Patty didn't scream. Instead, she looked at the deep cut into her stomach and felt as her innards began to tumble out. Blood ran down her shorts as her intestines spilled down her bare legs. Looking back at Dave and Meredith, her mouth opened in a silent expression of shock as they stood and stared back. That's when a second swing of the scythe caught her at the chest and yanked her back to the edge of the cornfield, and a flailing group of hands and arms reached from within the field to grab her, dragging her quickly behind the tightly clustered stalks of corn.

Meredith broke back into hysteria, screaming formlessly. Grabbing her by the arm, Dave pulled her away from the culvert and shouted, "Run!"

The huge truck had a noisy engine, but Conrad's voice was boisterous enough to talk over the loudest of engine rackets. "We're pretty close, kid. Just over the hill." Keith was captivated by this driver, who had been talking about everything from car repairs to his participation in the Battle of Nations, armored combat and endurance training. "It's a battle of brothers, kid! Honor and integrity mean everything. We don't reenact. We fight!"

The lit sign of the shop came into view and Keith breathed a sigh of relief. The rest of the gang was probably getting antsy by now; he'd been on the road with Conrad for about 20 minutes, but he knew that Joe had the patience of a gnat and Dave was likely getting stoned. He also knew that, even after getting the SUV gassed up, it would still take probably more than another two hours to get everyone dropped off and then get Brian and himself home. He wasn't excited at the prospect, but the shine of the overhead gas bays was at least a halfway mark towards getting this mess over with.

"Let's go, kid!" Conrad had already shut down the engine and jumped to the concrete by the door. Keith followed him as fast as he could, trying to figure out

where Conrad got this much stamina. A second man stepped out from behind the counter to get a look at Conrad and the boy who trailed behind him. "What have we here?" the man asked. "You're out after curfew, aren't you?"

Conrad laughed the big bellied laugh that Keith had gotten to hear several times during the drive. "This is Keith. He and his buddies ran out of gas about 20 miles back. Lucky for them I happened to be coming back from a tow or they'd probably still be back in the triangle. Keith, this is my partner, Claus."

Claus looked a lot like Conrad. Same stocky build, goatee, but a full head of brown hair instead of Conrad's imposing shaved dome. "The triangle? You are lucky, Keith. A lot of weird things going on out there at night. Lots of abandoned cars that lose their owners." He shuddered a little. "Conrad's probably told you that we've towed in a bunch of them that never get claimed."

Remembering that Conrad had mentioned the story of The Dutchman's Triangle made Keith suspicious. Were the two men messing with him? Was this like a jackalope hunt? The serious look on Claus's face seemed a little too intense to fake, and then he came around from the back of the counter and gave Conrad a huge hug and kiss. "Wait a second," Keith said hesitantly. "When you said you were partners, did you mean . . . well . . .'partners'?"

Again with the big, contagious laugh, Conrad chuckled, "Of course we are! What did you think we meant?"

"Wow," Keith took in a huge breath. He stared at the big couple, took in another deep breath and softly said, "My brother doesn't even know this. But I'm gay."

This time it was Claus who let out a hearty laugh. "You set off my gaydar as soon as you walked in the door, Keith." He turned

to Conrad. "You sure know how to find them. Now, what do we need to do here?"

Grabbing a pair of red plastic containers from one of the store shelves, Conrad decided, "I think five gallons will be enough to get them back here. Then they can fill up their gas hog and get the rest of the way back to New Jersey." Claus flipped a switch behind the counter. "Pumps are open." Keith followed Conrad out to the gas pumps and watched as the nozzle began pouring gasoline into the first receptacle.

"How did he know?" Keith asked.

"Know what?"

Keith shuffled his feet. "That I was gay?"

Instead of laughing, this time Conrad looked seriously at Keith. "You'll probably catch on yourself, sooner or later. But sometimes, in your mind, a little switch just pops and you'll know." He finished with the gas pump and was screwing the cap back on the second container. "Hey, I know. Telling people for the first time is tough. Look at me and Claus. I doubt anyone who stops in here during the day to get their cars worked on ever guesses. But here we are. And I knew it from the first time we saw each other. All it took was me getting the nerve to go and ask him."

Looking at the two gas cans on the ground, Keith switched topics. "What do I owe you for that?"

The laugh returned. "Nothing, kid. I think you just made our night." He picked up the containers and put them in the back of the truck. "Wait a minute. We'll need one more thing." He turned to go back in the store. Keith followed.

Claus gave him a wink. "So did he bore you with all his Battle of Nations stories?"

Conrad actually flushed a bit. "Well, it wasn't boring at all," Keith responded. "In fact, it sounds pretty intense."

"Oh it is," Conrad said, a little sheepish this time. "But let me show you something." There was a second set of doors in a hallway along the counter. Pulling them open and switching on the lights, Keith took in a trove of what looked like something out of a medieval movie. Round, silver metal shields. Huge helmets with slits for eyes. Swords and axes were mounted on the walls. "This is it," he proudly announced. "My armory."

Claus came in behind Keith. "Don't get him started," he warned. "You'll never get back to your friends." The warning didn't stop Conrad for a moment. He took one of the swords down from the wall, unsheathed it, and handed it to Keith. Keith was surprised at just how heavy it really was. He also noticed that the blade wasn't sharp enough to cut anything.

Conrad noticed Keith's observation, too, and said, "We never use anything that would intentionally hurt someone. We fight for real, but there are no enemies, no anger. If someone takes a hard shot, my hard shot, and remains of good spirit, then he has the honor of calling me equal and himself a man of knightly mettle. Likewise, if he gives me a hard shot with fair but entirely violent intent and I stay in the fight and of good cheer, then I have earned the right to take his hand in respect and friendship."

"I warned you," Claus said with a prideful smile. "He means every word of it, too."

Conrad reached up and took another, broader leather casing off the wall. "One more," he said, "but be careful. This one is the real thing. This blade is sharpened to a diamond's fineness." He slid it from the leather, then handed it, handle extended, to Keith. It was even heavier than the first one. Now he knew why Conrad seemed to have so much endless energy. If he was carrying these weapons and armor, then still physically fighting while wearing it, he had to be stronger than an ox. "Want to show that one to your

friends?" Conrad asked with a twinkle in his eyes. The broadness of the sword sure was impressive. At the very least, Keith figured, Brian would get a charge from it. He nodded "yes" and got another one of Conrad's boisterous laughs. "All right then! Let's go get you a full tank." Taking the sturdy leather case and meticulously fastening the safety straps closed to hold the sword inside, Conrad snagged a funnel off the shelf and bounded back to the truck, sheathed sword in hand.

Keith could hardly keep up with the man, but he scooted outside as well. As he was running across the pavement, he heard Claus call out behind him, "Take care of him for me. Don't get into any battles!" Conrad laughed again and started up the truck for their return trip.

This time, Susan was absolutely certain that she'd heard Meredith screaming. She was also more than positive she'd heard Dave yelling something from a short distance away. The full moon wasn't quite bright enough to clearly illuminate that far ahead, but her ears were not deceiving her. Grabbing hold of Brian, she whispered in fear, "Did you hear it that time?"

Even over his previous misgivings, Brian couldn't deny a series of continuous screams, and what sounded like Dave yelling above it. He could also tell, like Susan, that the sounds weren't far away. He jumped into the SUV and turned the key enough to bring the headlights on. There was no sign of anything ahead of the car except the omnipresent corn stalks and pasture, but there was some sort of noise that seemed to be coming out of the cornfield. Susan was clinging to the door, looking at Brian with terror on her face. "I don't know what it is," Brain said in an urgent, soft voice, "but I don't like the sound of it."

Susan stayed silent as Brian honked the horn a few times, hoping that Meredith, Joe, Patty and Dave would hear it and get back to the SUV. Still, no one came and there were no more sounds from his friends. He crawled back to the back of the vehicle and pulled the athletic bag from under the seat. Taking out a pair of aluminum softball bats, he handed one off to Susan, and, still speaking softly, told her to keep her eyes out for anything that looked wrong. He then remembered what Conrad had warned them about before he took Keith for gasoline. "The Dutchman's Triangle," he said. Was this what he was talking about? He got out of the SUV and stood with Susan, side by side and against the side of the SUV, breathing as silently as they could.

There were more sounds from the cornfield. Shadows. Brian could see shadows. They walked out into the road, but, he thought, not a walk as much as a shuffle. There were also too many of them. This wasn't Patty, Meredith, Dave or Joe. He heard Susan gasp as the bodies moved into the range of the headlights. She pulled herself tight to Brian. These were definitely not their friends. They wore black, ragged clothing. Their limbs seemed to dangle at the sides of their torn clothes. It even looked like there were children among them. But the real horror came when the group came close enough to see faces. White, scarred faces. Men and women, stumbling towards them. Skin that peeled back or hung off from their necks. The long beards, mottled with pus and . . .

Susan screamed. She recognized that along with the oozing rot that was permeating the beards was blood.

Brian spun around and jumped on the hood of the SUV. "Come on!" he shouted, grabbing Susan's hands and pulling her up with him. Grasping the roof rack in one hand and the softball bat in the other, he hoisted himself to the roof of the SUV and pulled Susan up beside him. Whatever they were, they didn't look like they were able to climb anything. They gathered around the front of the SUV, but not looking at Brian or Susan. They stooped over each other, staring into the headlights. Keeping

a finger to his lips, Brian signaled to Susan to try and keep quiet. Shaking as much as she could without falling off the roof, Susan understood. The shouts, headlights and horn had drawn them near, but so far they hadn't noticed the two teens hiding just over their heads. If they just stayed still long enough, maybe these things would wander off.

Except Susan just couldn't stop shaking in fear. She was barely able to handle the reek emanating off this crowd of bodies surrounding the headlamp beams, and the dreadful groans and grunts they were making. She tried to slip herself just a little closer to Brian, to get away from these things, these awful, rotting things, as she pressed herself to Brian's side. As she did, she slipped just the tiniest fraction of her grip on her softball bat, and it tapped just enough to make a barely audible clink. The groans and shuffling came to a sudden halt. The broken bodies slowly raised their heads in the direction of the sound, and their eyes to where Susan and Brian were crouching. Suddenly there was a flailing of arms around the edges of the SUV's roof, threatening but not quite able to get to the center where the two teens huddled, terrified.

The screaming girl had once again managed to escape, but Ezekiel was still confident. Usually the meat had to be forced to stop along the highway, often by his flock in the center of the road. When the car was drawn to a stop, the occupants were easily pulled out and into the hungry arms of the assembled. These young people had fallen into Ezekiel's hands without effort by virtue of their giant vehicle stalling exactly where he could lead his followers to food. The screaming girl and her male companion had been sent running through the pasture towards the cloister, and the other two were keeping to the vehicle. They were divided. All the easier to conquer.

As for the girl, he had pulled into the cornfield; the hungry had already ripped her flesh down to the bone. Despite having consumed the young man just minutes before, they were still ravenous, pulling at the remaining scraps of uneaten entrails, blood dripping like hot sauce from their lips. There was something strange that Ezekiel noticed this time, though. The screams of the girl and the shouts of the boy had caught the attention of members of his clan, with several of them sniffing the air in an attempt to ascertain where the sounds were originating from. Some had even staggered to their feet, moving in the direction of the sounds. Better than half of them seemed to making their way out from the corn and onto the roadway, while the remaining hunched over the body of the second girl, pulling what little edible strips of skin clung to her body.

He cried out to the wandering, demanding that they obey his orders and return. Ezekiel knew that the scent of food could overwhelm their need to stay within the ranks of their family. Still, he ordered, "Stop!" as they ignored his scythe brandishing demands. Ezekiel sighed. It wouldn't matter in the end: he would ultimately gather his assembly before dawn, their stomachs filled by this night's killings, and they'd make their way back to their cave.

But then a new set of sounds came from the roadway. The other two by the vehicle had turned on the headlights and began calling to their friends. Even the pull of warm meat wasn't enough to stop his flock this time. They gathered on the roadway and began making their way towards the lights and honking. If they got a whiff of the two teenagers at the vehicle, Ezekiel realized, his assemblage would be split and out of his control. He watched as he counted seven of his assembled beginning to make their way towards the sound and light. "This is not good," he thought. He couldn't have two sides of his charges wandering apart from each other. He had to think quickly. He knew where the vehicle was, but wasn't sure where the better number of his group had gone, other than

in the general direction of the cloister. In a snap decision, Ezekiel reckoned that he knew where the vehicle would be and it wasn't going to leave the roadway, while the larger number was wandering freely and that was the greater of his problems. He gathered his scythe and trotted down in the general direction of the new barn.

Meredith and Dave were running mostly blind through the moonlight towards what looked like a barn in the middle of a field full of houses. There were trees around the houses, but no lights were on. Meredith was screaming for help, but Dave was more worried that whatever the things were that killed Joe and Patty would follow them if they made too much noise. The high he had going back at the culvert was completely shocked out of his system by this point, and he kept trying to signal to Meredith to quiet down. They were against the wall of the barn, and Dave looked frantically around for anything that would offer protection.

The barn door was easily opened, but Dave figured if he could open it, so could their pursuers. There was also a long, locking bar across the front of the door, which also meant that whatever he could unlock could be used to lock them in. Then he spied a ladder. "Meredith, come here. Let's get this against the wall; I think there's an opening near the top." Jostling the ladder for position, he propped the ladder against the opening, which he assumed was an entrance to a hayloft. There was an overhanging bracket from which a block and tackle was hanging. If they could get up there and pull the ladder with them, Dave figured, they'd be safe.

They dragged the ladder to the barn's wall and rested it against what looked like the opening. Dave scurried up the ladder, motioning Meredith to follow. But she kept staring across the field, as if hypnotized by their pursuers. "Meredith!" Dave whispered as loudly as he could, "Get up here!" Dave could now see the shadowy figures stumbling towards them,

TACO

with Meredith staring like a girl trapped in the headlights. He shimmied back down the ladder and grabbed Meredith by the arm. "Move it!"

Jostled back to her senses, Meredith jumped on the ladder as Dave rushed back to the opening. He pulled into the opening and turned himself around to help Meredith climb to within arm's reach. But the figures had reached the base of the ladder to the point where Dave could finally see them. Even worse, he could smell them. The stench was like a day at the beach when the dead fish would wash up on the shore. The people at the ladder didn't look right, either. They were hideously pale, skin drawn tight across what he could only guess were faces. They looked like faces, but things were missing or out of place: noses seemed to have fallen across mouths and the hair was pulled away from their scalps. These things, he thought with a shot of terror, had killed Patty right in front of them. They gathered at the base of the ladder and started to shake it. Dave extended his arm as far as he could, but Meredith had frozen in fear, the ladder rocking under her.

"Grab my hand! Meredith, grab me!" Dave thrust his hands down to where Meredith could reach, and she clutched him by the wrists. "Come on! Come up!" Dave exhorted, when he suddenly saw him. He wasn't like these rotting men and women gathered around the ladder. He walked with an upright stance, and his clothes were dark, but whole, unlike the tatters of their original attackers. And Dave could see his eyes. They were bright with purpose, and he pushed those bodies at the ladder aside. Dave could also see that he was holding a large scythe, and then did the unthinkable. He knocked the ladder out from under Meredith.

She cried out and tightened her grasp on Dave's arms. Dave tried to pull Meredith up, but he could see the dark man pick up his scythe and take a swipe at Meredith. The scythe Dave saw that split Patty's

stomach open back at the culvert. He pulled up on Meredith's arms even harder, shouting, "Don't let go!" The scythe took another swing at Meredith, skimming through the space between her legs and just barely catching her cheerleader skirt. He even saw that stupid teddybear on the ground getting trampled by this madman and these things that were surrounding him. Dave double-clutched Meredith's wrists in another effort to pull her over the lip of the entrance. Dangling over the edge of the loft, Meredith kept kicking, trying to knock the sharp blade away from her body, her feet and legs kicking, kicking. The crazy dark man swung again, but this time, he caught the back of Meredith's sweater and cut a line down her back. Even if he couldn't see the gash, Dave knew that it drew blood, and he felt Meredith's grip loosen.

"No! No! You're not going down," Dave shouted. He gave one more pull as hard as he could, but this time he saw the scythe swing and drive in just below Meredith's belt line. She gave one more hysterical scream, and slipped out of Dave's grip. Hanging over the side of the loft opening, he saw the dark man step aside to allow those around him to fall upon Meredith, and sickened at the sight. The malformed people who seemed to follow the man with the scythe set on Meredith and began ripping her open where the tool had torn her back and opened her below the waist. Her cheerleader sweater was soaking in blood as the arms and hands flailed away. "Dear God," Dave thought, "those things are *eating* her!" He then saw the dark man pull up the ladder and try and prop it against the loft opening again. Dave understood: the bastard was going to come after him and feed him to those monsters. He flipped over on his back and kicked at the ladder every time the dark man tried to lay the top of the ladder against where Dave was trapped. Dammit, he thought, where were Keith and Brian?

They'd only been gone for less than an hour, but Keith thought it was

taking forever. Despite Conrad's jovial disposition, it was getting later than he had planned, even with the extra time of not taking toll roads. He just wanted to get back on the highway and head for home. Conrad, though, seemed to have an endless wellspring of energy. "We should be coming up on your car anytime, kid," he exclaimed. "Just around this bend." He slowed the rumbling truck down in anticipation of spotting the SUV, but even he gasped when his attention was drawn to the scene along the side of the road. There were nine people gathered around the SUV, with Brian and Susan crouching together on the roof, and Brian swinging a softball bat anytime one of them tried to reach over the edge.

"Mother Mary and Joseph," Conrad muttered. "I never believed the stories until now."

"What stories?" Keith asked, his voice rising to a panic.

Conrad reached behind his seat, to where his sword was sheathed. "Frigging Mennonite Zombies, boy." He pulled the sheath away and let the truck inch closer to the frightened Brian and Susan and their undead attackers. "It's time to slice some zombie heads." Conrad leapt from the truck, sword extended. Keith could only watch as the big man started roaring, swinging, catching the staggering figures at the neck and making their heads fly into the air. One by one, Conrad dispatched the zombies, ooze spurting from the neck of each as Conrad's sword struck each with deadly purpose. Keith watched in astonishment as the figures, large and small, fell to the impact of Conrad's weapon and their heads struck the roadway, rolling like bowling balls. He could also see Brain and Susan, huddling in shock as Conrad's sword made short work of the seven figures that had been trying to reach them from the sides of the SUV.

There were soon nothing more than severed bodies oozing slime and rotting heads scattered around the SUV. Conrad held his sword with both fists clamped around the hilt, backing slowly towards the big truck. "Don't move!" he bellowed at Susan and Brian. He jumped in the truck and drew it alongside the SUV. "Jump in the back, now!" Brian and Susan wasted no time, leaping into the truck bed.

Keith turned around and looked at the fear in his brother's eyes. "Where is everyone?" he asked through the panel in the truck's rear window.

"I don't know," Brian gasped. "All I know is that I heard Dave and Meredith yelling for help and running through the field," he said, pointing down towards where the barn and houses were shrouded by darkness.

"Hang on to your asses," Conrad shouted, "we're going off-road." The tires spun on the gravel as Conrad's truck jumped off the shoulder and started heading towards the cloister. The Moon was still bright, but not enough for Keith to make out much more than the trees and houses that seemed to all have their lights out. Other than the headlights, there still wasn't much else to see. Then Conrad slammed on the brakes. "Oh, shit," he muttered under his breath. Keith turned to see the side of the barn, and where more of the zombies had gathered, and then he saw, for the first time, the dark man who the undead seemed to gather around. He was pushing a ladder at a wall, but it kept falling back, no matter how hard he tried.

"It's them," Keith exclaimed, "it's gotta be them!"

"Make some noise," Conrad commanded. "Draw them away from the barn." He pressed down hard on the truck's horn, and it was a loud one. "Brian and Susan started shouting and banging the aluminum bats on the truck bed. Keith looked over at the wall. It was working.

Whatever had their attention before, they were being drawn away. The mob started to stumble towards them. "Keep it up," exclaimed Conrad, "keep making noise!" He shifted the truck in reverse and let it inch away from the barn. As the remaining zombies lurched in the direction of the headlights and noise, the truck slowly drew them back from the barn. Inches turned to feet, feet into yards, with Brian and Susan still beating the truck bed and Conrad honking the horn. But Keith noticed that the man in the black clothes, the one with the ladder, wasn't with them. He couldn't figure out why he didn't follow the rest of the herd. Keith also noticed that, while these creatures only staggered and stumbled, the dark man was agile enough to lift a ladder, several times. A red light went off in his head, but he couldn't quite place it.

Suddenly, Conrad spun the truck around, and did a fast circle around the barn. The ladder was on the ground, but then they all heard a shout for help. Looking up, they saw Dave in the hayloft. When Keith opened the truck door, they also saw the bloody, dismembered remains of Meredith, torn apart like the oversized teddybear on the ground next to her. Entrails were pulled across the ground, organs tossed about like pebbles. Susan spotted the body parts and leaned over the truck, beginning to throw up.

Brian jumped over the back of the truck and grabbed the ladder. "We don't have much time," he exclaimed, propping the ladder to reach Dave. "Get down here, man, fast!" As Dave slid down the ladder as fast as he could, Keith felt the welling of panic again. Looking back at what was left of Meredith, he asked Dave, "Where is everybody else?"

Dave was so pale that Brian and Keith almost thought he'd become a zombie himself. "I saw Patty and Meredith get killed by these things; Meredith said they got Joe. Man, we've got to get out of here. Like, right now! And there was some crazy guy with the ladder, trying to come up after me."

There was a thump from the back of the truck, and they all turned to see Conrad, holding the two plastic canisters of gasoline. "Not yet." Everyone stopped and stared. "We're going to burn these bitches."

"How do you think we're going to do that?" Dave questioned.

Conrad held up the gas cans. "First they're going to march into this barn, and then we're going to shut them in and burn this mother down. But we've gotta move fast. They'll be here any second." Conrad lifted the lock bar away from the door. "Keith, you're going to get behind this and shove it closed when they get inside, then bar the door shut. You," he said, pointing to Dave, "are going to run through the barn ahead of them and dump this gas. I'll bring the truck around to the other side with Brian and you," he gestured towards Susan. "I saw another door just like this one on the other side. When you get done with the gasoline, we set the thing on fire and bar the door with those things inside. Anything gets through eats my sword. It's not much of a plan, but it's all we've got right now." He eyed the four teens intensely. "Ready?"

Dave held out his hands for the gas containers. "I'm a go. Everyone else?"

Keith was already getting behind the barn door and Dave positioned himself behind the wall with the gas. "You two, in the back of the truck. Start banging when we open the door on the other side; let's go!" As Susan and Brian climbed back into the truck bed, Conrad looked at Keith and said, "You ready for this, kid?" Keith nodded, and then silently pointed. The first of the flock was coming into view. "Everybody in place — now!" He jumped into the truck and spun it around towards the opposite side of the barn, and threw open the opposing barn doors. The headlights blazed through the barn like a train at the long end of a tunnel. Brian and Susan began banging on the truck bed as Conrad piled on the horn blasts.

The bodies began to turn their attention toward the lights and the racket. Keith hid behind the open fold of the door, holding his breath. He knew that Dave must be doing the same thing. That was when the first of the zombies staggered to the barn door, and he heard Dave mutter "Here, piggy, piggy, piggy." Keith could smell the first splash of the gasoline as the crowd stumbled past him and towards Dave and the noises. The smell of the dead and the gasoline was nearly overwhelming, and Keith had to use all the control he had not to cough or make any other sound. He thought of Susan vomiting over Meredith's remains, and knew he couldn't allow his revulsion to take over his senses. The shuffling and stench continued toward the truck lights, noise and Dave's baiting them. Keith couldn't count them, but he could hear the dragging shuffle of their feet and the sickening gurgling sounds they made from this close by. But then he realized the unholy clump of these things had passed the threshold of the barn doors. He shoved them shut and lifted the cross bar into place, solidly locking anything inside, headed towards Dave and the truck. Still, he couldn't shake the thought of man in the black clothes — all the bodies who went passed him had torn up clothing and rotting skin; that man with the ladder was wearing what looked like a suit. Dave said he was trying to use the ladder. No time, he thought, no time. He began sprinting around the side of the barn to where the truck was waiting.

Dave was splashing gasoline on the floorboards as the mob moved towards him, just feet away. Good Lord, he thought, they stink. He kept backing up as quickly as he could when he heard Keith shove the door closed and lock it. Muttering over again "Here piggy, piggy, piggy," as he turned to try and run the last few yards to the opening where Brian, Susan and Conrad were waiting. But as he spun, he felt his sneaker catch on a raised board and felt his ankle give a hard twist. As he sprawled to the floor, he let go of one of the gas cans, which went spinning across the floor, spraying gasoline like a water sprinkler all around him. He cried out in pain as he hit the boards, and realized that he'd turned his ankle. But those things were just feet away and he had to get up and run. Even more important, he had to light the matches in his shirt pocket. He tried to get up, but yelped again as his leg gave out from under him. The only thing he could do was try and crawl on all fours to get away from the zombies, now drawing even closer.

On his hands and knees, Dave tried to scurry towards safety, but even that wasn't fast enough. He could hear Brian and Susan egging him on, calling to him to hurry, faster, faster. That's when he felt the first of the creatures grab his leg — his leg with the sprained ankle. His body exploded in pain as his foot bent in the wrong direction, in the grip of one of those things. He threw the remaining gas can at it and it let go. The gas began spilling out into a puddle around him and his attackers. By then, others had caught up and were reaching out for his limbs, and Dave realized it was too late. He pulled the little box of wooden matches from his shirt pocket and tried to fumble one out.

Now one of those creatures had his leg, but this time the one that wasn't hurt. Dave kicked as hard as he could and shook this one off. He kept trying to get a match loose, and the irony of a flash memory hit him; was it only just minutes ago that he was using these for Patty and him to get high? In that moment, he again heard the cries from Brian and Susan from the barn door, frantically calling for him to get up and get out. Dave turned on his stomach and held out the box of matches. That was right when one of the monsters caught hold of his leg and sank his teeth into Dave's jeans, tearing away the denim and into the flesh. Dave screamed again, and this time let the box of matches fly through the air.

Brian saw it happen, too, and felt an adrenal explosion. He rushed past Conrad and Susan, scooping up the matchbox and grabbing Dave by the arm. "Come on, buddy, come on," he barked out, "get the hell out of here!" But even with Brian pulling on his arms, Dave couldn't shake off the zombie ripping at his leg, and then others began to catch up. The putrid stench was on him; all he could do was feel their rotting hands grabbing him while he spun and twisted to get free.

"Get the matches and get out!" He screamed at Brian. It was the last coherent thing he said, as more of the zombies had fallen on him and were tearing him open. Brian stood, paralyzed for just a heartbeat by the horror of the sight, then snapped out of it. He could hear Conrad and Susan shouting from the barn door, yelling for him. Swiftly scooping up the matchbox, Brian struck one against the flint and threw it towards the empty gas can, then watched as the flames whooshed across the wooden floors and to where Dave was splayed out, with the zombies pulling and biting down at his limbs. The trails of gasoline that had been spilled and had spun across the barn began to flicker, then catch in the accelerant and sawdust left behind from the morning's construction. Dave's screams were joined by a chorus of high-pitched, groaning wails as the zombies' decaying clothing got caught up in the surrounding whirlwind of fire. Turning and running as hard as he could, Brian broke for the door.

As soon as he was out, Conrad and Susan pushed the doors closed and dropped the locking wooden bar into place. The heat was already intensifying as Brian backed away, sweating, leaning with his hands on his knees, trying to both catch his breath and take in the horror. He was hit by the repulsive realization that he'd just set his friend on fire while seeing him being clawed through the skin by those things that were now burning to their deaths inside

the barn. Keith came around from the opposite corner of the barn, also hearing the wailing and moans from within the burning structure. Conrad raised his arm in the air and hailed Keith. "It's done — we got 'em." But they were turned towards Keith, and they didn't spot that Ezekiel had come around the opposite corner and was coming up on the still hunched-over Brian.

"Brian, look out!" he shouted, but Ezekiel had already grabbed Brian by the hair and had slipped his scythe's sharp under-blade against Brian's neck. Susan and Conrad heard the sound of Brian's gasp and turned to see Ezekiel with one arm pulling back Brian's head and the other high on the scythe's handle.

"You took my family," Ezekiel snarled. "You killed my flock!"

Conrad had both hands on the hilt of his sword and was already in a defensive stance. Susan screamed and Keith bolted to the center of the standoff. "He's my brother . . . don't hurt him."

"Brother," scoffed Ezekiel. "You say brother when you kill brothers and sisters, fathers and sons." He turned toward Conrad, snarling. "And you, swordsman. How many of my kin did you behead and leave on the roadway?" Conrad took a step forward; Ezekiel countered by moving his grip higher on the handle of the scythe, pressing the blade into the skin at Brian's neck. "A head for a head. I'd call that justice, wouldn't you?"

When Susan saw Brian choke as the blade pulled tighter, she shouted, "Don't!"

Ezekiel turned to her, the fury consuming his face. "Pretty lady, this is your boyfriend, no?" When Susan didn't reply, Ezekiel smirked. "So young. Never to have beautiful children. Not what you thought when you and your friends stopped in my village, is it?" He stepped forward, pushing Brian and the razor-sharp blade away from the burning barn and towards his throat. Staring back at Brian, Ezekiel, pulled back harder on Brian's hair, exposing the neck even more. Turning now to Keith, he kept his menacing tone as he taunted, "What will you tell your mother and father? Tonight I killed a family by burning them alive?"

Keith edged forward, even as he heard Conrad warning him to stand back. "Your 'family' killed my friends. They were eating their skin off. What sort of family is this?" Behind him, he could sense Conrad inching in equal distance just behind him. The reflections of the flames from the barn were visible in his sword. Keith was hoping he could close enough of a distance between the dark man holding Brian and Conrad's weapon that he could get a clean enough shot that Brian could get free.

Keeping pace with Keith and Conrad's maneuvering, Ezekiel roared, "It's *my* family." He let the blade dig a little cut into Brian's neck, forcing Brian to let out a little gasping cry. A trickle of blood began to ooze down Brian's collar. Susan let out another scream. Conrad moved towards his left as Keith moved just a step to his right. Brian's eyes darted back and forth between Conrad and Keith, and Keith could see that Brian was visibly shivering in fear of the scythe cutting any deeper. But even as they tried to split and circle him, Ezekiel stepped back. "Brother for brother. Head for head, no?" he quizzed, still keeping his safe distance, the fire now casting mad shadows around their dangerous dance. The heat was intense and the cries of the burning had ceased.

Ezekiel shouted out again, "Brother for brother!" He paused again. "Blood for blood!" With a swiftness that Keith did not expect from a man who looked to be so elderly, he rammed Brian's neck down onto the cutting edge of the scythe and pulled the handle across, slicing deep into the flesh. Brian had little time to do anything but gasp as the artery began spraying blood across Ezekiel, spurting

hard enough to splatter Keith in the face. Keith didn't even see as Conrad lunged forward, burying his sword into the dark man's rib cage with a hard swing. Keith could hear the bones crack as the old man went down.

Ezekiel dropped his scythe and broke into a sad, hysterical laughter. "I am not the only Shepherd," he called out to the three of them.

Susan had rushed up to Brian, cradling his head in her arms and crying, the seeping blood running across her jeans and blouse. Keith rushed to her side, trying to get her up and away. Conrad was already urging them to get to the truck. "Come on," Keith said to her in a hushed voice. "We've got to get out of here and call the police. We have to leave now."

She gathered her wits and got up slowly, Keith helping her to the truck. Conrad was standing on the truck's running board, slapping the roof of the car. Keith could see on his shirt where the dark man's blood had stained Conrad after dealing the blow to the man's chest. "Come on, guys!" he exhorted. "We need to get the hell out of here!" Conrad reached out to Susan, lifting her to the middle of the truck's back seat; Keith was already inside the passenger door. He could see the blood-covered sword as Conrad floored the gas pedal. Dirt and grass flew as the truck lurched, first in reverse and then speeding towards the highway and away from the burning barn.

Ezekiel was on the ground, propped up on his scythe handle. He heard and saw the Swordsman's truck tear up the sod and race away. He could feel the deep wound in his side, and the wrenching pain of the broken bones as the bleeding turned his white shirt crimson dark. The dead boy was face down on the ground near him, just out of reach. His blood was now comingling with that from the boy's slit throat. The fire from the barn he'd helped build just that morning was still lighting

up the area around him when he heard
another voice calling his name. He turned
to see another man, dressed traditionally
as he was, and holding a scythe. A flowing
brown beard rested on the man's white
shirt. Ezekiel turned, as gently as he
could, towards the other man's voice.

"Brother Lester," he moaned. "I have lost
my flock. They have taken them away from
me." It hurt him now to even talk, his voice
rasping through the blood in his chest.
"They cut them apart on the highway
and burned the rest of them alive." From
behind Brother Lester, Ezekiel could hear
the shuffling. Coming down to one knee,
Brother Lester took Ezekiel's hand and
clasped it in his.

"Don't fear, my old friend," Lester said in
a soothing voice. They will be cleaned and
carried away before the sun has a chance
to come up. Our community will keep its
secret. Brother Ezekiel, you were a good
shepherd. Your flock followed you faith-
fully. But you weren't the last shepherd."

Ezekiel could feel his mind fading. "No,
Brother Lester," he wheezed. "And mine
was not the only flock." From behind
Brother Lester, Ezekiel could hear the
shuffling. As his eyes dimmed, he could
feel the solitary bite into his arm. By the
warmth of the remaining fire, he knew he
would be part of Brother Lester's flock
soon enough.